P9-DME-612

No Biting, Louise

By Margie Palatini

Illustrated by

Matthew Reinhart

KATHERINE TEGEN BOOKS

An Imprint of HarperCollins*Publishers*

No Biting, Louise
Text copyright © 2007 by Margie Palatini
Illustrations copyright © 2007 by Matthew Reinhart

Manufactured in China.
All rights reserved. No part of this book may be used or reproduced in any manner whatsoever without written permission except in the case of brief quotations embodied in critical articles and reviews. For information address HarperCollins Children's Books, a division of HarperCollins Publishers, 195 Broadway, New York, NY 10007.
www.harpercollinschildrens.com

Library of Congress Cataloging-in-Publication Data
Palatini, Margie.
No biting, Louise / by Margie Palatini; illustrated by Matthew Reinhart. — 1st ed.
p. cm.
Summary: At the urging of her family, Louise, a young alligator, tries hard to kick her biting habit.
ISBN-13: 978-0-06-052627-6 (trade bdg.) — ISBN-10: 0-06-052627-0 (trade bdg.)
ISBN-13: 978-0-06-052628-3 (lib. bdg.) — ISBN-10: 0-06-052628-9 (lib. bdg.)
1. Alligators—Fiction. 2. Teeth—Fiction. I. Reinhart, Matthew, ill. II. Title.
PZ7.P1755Nob 2007 2006029389
[E]—dc22

Typography by Carla Weise

14 15 16 LEO 10 9 8 7 6 5 4
❖
First Edition

For my dear friend Louise

—M.P.

To my sister, Erin,

who *is* Louise

—M.R.

Louise was a delight.

A darling.

An absolute dear.

Most of the time.

However,

upon occasion . . .

she could be just a tad . . .

trying.

"No biting, Louise!"

Yes. There was that tendency to . . .
how to put it?

Gnaw?

On everything. Everyone. Everywhere.

"OOOOO oooh!"

"EEEeeeeeee!"

"Ooooowwwwwww!"

"No biting,
Louise!"

Louise promised Mother:
Absolutely no more biting.
Nope.
Never.
Ever.

Mother was not pleased with Louise.

Louise was sorry.

She was really, really, truly quite sorry.

It was just that she was so proud of her new gleaming-white baby choppers.

Try as she might—
and she tried,
she truly tried—

Louise could not resist the temptation to nibble.

Louise meant no harm in a chomp or two now and then. Surely everyone knew that.

They did not.

Except—for Grandmama Sadie.

"Nana's little love," she cooed and hugged. "Tsk. Tsk. Tsk. Such bother over a little biting. A few nibbles. A smattering of some carefree chomps. Such pooh!"

"Not to worry," said Grandmama. "I am quite sure, totally positive, mark my words, that this is only a phase my little joy is going through. She will outgrow it!"

"OOOOOOWWWW!"

"And hopefully . . .

soon."

And . . . **she did!**

Thankfully. Most gratefully. Louise did indeed.

Just as Grandmama Sadie predicted, all in good time there was no more biting from Louise.

The problem now—

was something else entirely.

"Chew, Louise, chew," instructed Mother. "My dear, you must remember to chew everything well before you swallow."

BURP.

Louise was going to
have to work on that.